Dear Reader,

We're excited to present this book to you as a gift from us to take home, read and enjoy. *I've Lost My Cat* is a story of a boy who has lost his cat and he cannot seem to find it. His friends bring him many wonderful animals that they believe look like his cat, but none of them do. Will he ever find his furry friend? You will have to read this book to discover the answer!

All of us at TD are proud to provide this book to you as part of the TD Grade One Book Giveaway, one of several children's reading programs we support each year. Every Grade One student in Canada will receive a copy of *I've Lost My Cat* this year. We encourage you to visit your local library to discover the magical world of books.

Have fun reading!

Ed Clark

President and CEO
TD Bank Group

Dear Kids and Parents,

The Canadian Children's Book Centre is proud to partner with TD Bank Group to give you *I've Lost My Cat,* this year's TD Grade One Book Giveaway selection. For over ten years, we have given every Grade One student a wonderful Canadian children's book through this program so that they discover what a passion for reading and a love of books can bring to their lives.

Please take this book home to read with your parents. We think you will all love this story of a boy who thinks he has lost his cat and whose friends try to help him find it.

We hope that you and your parents will also enjoy reading some of the other great Canadian award-winning books listed in the back of this book.

We wish you much happy reading now and for always.

Charlotte Teeple

Charlotte Teeple

Executive Director
The Canadian Children's Book Centre

The Canadian Children's Book Centre

The Canadian Children's Book Centre

Over 500,000 Grade One students across Canada will receive a copy of this book, *I've Lost My Cat*, through the annual TD Grade One Book Giveaway Program, administered by the Canadian Children's Book Centre (CCBC) and funded by TD Bank Group.

The Canadian Children's Book Centre is a national, not-for-profit organization that promotes the reading, writing and illustrating of Canadian children's books. The CCBC provides programs, resources, materials and activities that are used by teachers, librarians, authors, illustrators, publishers, booksellers and parents.

Best Books for Kids & Teens is the Canadian Children's Book Centre's semi-annual selection guide to the best new Canadian books, magazines, audio and video. Each year, hundreds of recently published books and other resources are evaluated and selected by jury committees from across the country. *Best Books for Kids & Teens* highlights the best Canadian books to buy, borrow and read, making it a terrific resource for anyone who wants to make informed selections for young readers.

Canadian Children's Book News, the CCBC's quarterly magazine, reviews books, interviews authors and illustrators, profiles publishers and bookstores, informs and updates readers about issues affecting children's education and reading and provides information and news about the world of children's books in Canada.

The Canadian Children's Book Centre organizes TD Canadian Children's Book Week, the largest annual celebration of Canadian books and reading in schools and libraries across Canada. Each spring, during TD Book Week, Canadian authors, illustrators and storytellers travel across the country, from coast to coast and up to the Arctic, visiting schools, libraries, community centres and bookstores to talk about their books with young readers. TD Book Week also inspires many independent activities and local celebrations of Canadian children's books and their creators.

The CCBC co-ordinates six major children's literature awards with cash prizes totalling over $120,000 including the TD Canadian Children's Literature Award for the most distinguished English and French-language books of the year, the Marilyn Baillie Picture Book Award, the Norma Fleck Award for Canadian Children's Non-Fiction, the Geoffrey Bilson Award for Historical Fiction for Young People, the John Spray Mystery Award and the Monica Hughes Award for Science Fiction and Fantasy.

For more information on the Canadian Children's Book Centre and the TD Grade One Book Giveaway Program, please visit our website at www.bookcentre.ca.

The Canadian Children's Book Centre
Bringing Canadian books and young readers together

The Canadian Children's Book Centre, 40 Orchard View Blvd., Suite 217 Toronto, Ontario M4R 1B9
Telephone: 416 975-0010, Fax: 416 975-8970, Email: info@bookcentre.ca

Special edition prepared for the TD Grade One Book Giveaway
Program.

This edition is published by special arrangement with the
Canadian Children's Book Centre and TD Bank Group for free
distribution to Grade One children across Canada in celebration
of the 2012 TD Canadian Children's Literature Awards.

Library and Archives Canada Cataloguing in Publication

Béha, Philippe
[J'ai perdu mon chat. English]
I've lost my cat / written and illustrated by Philippe Béha ;
translated by Julia Beck.

Translation of: J'ai perdu mon chat.
Published in celebration of the 2012 TD Canadian Children's Literature
Awards.
ISBN 978-0-929095-78-3

I. Beck, Julia, 1942- II. Canadian Children's Book Centre. III. Title.
IV. Title: J'ai perdu mon chat. English.

PS8553.E398J3413 2012   jC843'.54   C2012-901982-8

Printed and bound in Canada by Friesens Corporation
Also available in French: J'ai perdu mon chat
ISBN 978-0-929095-78-3 (English)
ISBN 978-0-929095-80-6 (French)

The Canadian Children's Book Centre
40 Orchard View Blvd., Suite 217
Toronto, Ontario M4R 1B9
www.bookcentre.ca

Les éditions Imagine
4446, boul. Saint-Laurent, 7e étage
Montréal (Québec) H2W 1Z5
Courriel : info@editionsimagine.com
Site Internet : www.editionsimagine.com

Philippe Beha

Translated by Julia Beck

I've Lost My Cat

black

yellow

white

very round

really cute

To my mother.
Philippe Beha

The Canadian Children's Book Centre

Oh, No! I've lost my cat, he's round, he's cute,

he's yellow, black and white, his name is Greyling
and he's nowhere in sight.

I've found your cat, all yellow, black and white.
He was lost and crying in fright.

That's not my cat, that's a leopard!
But thanks, he can stay in my backyard.

Here's your cat, all round and cute.
He was wandering around and about.

That's not my cat, that's a pig!
But thanks, he can stay in my house.

I've brought you your cat, all grey and round.
He was sleeping on the balcony.

That's not my cat, that's an elephant!
But thanks, he can stay with me.

I've caught your cat, all yellow and black.
He was hopping on the sidewalk.

That's not my cat, that's a canary! But thanks,
I've got a place where he can sing and squawk.

As soon as I called "Greyling" your cat followed me
all the way home.

That's not my cat, that's a sheep! But thanks,
I've got a place where he can roam.

I've brought back your cat, all white and black.
He was waddling about.

That's not my cat, that's a penguin!
But thanks, I'll find him a place to hang out.

I've caught your cat, all round, yellow and black.
He wasn't far.

That's not my cat, that's a fish! But thanks,
he can swim in my pickle jar.

Then today, I saw a yellow dog, a white mouse,
a yellow, black and white beetle and a black hen.

I was also given a round grey hat and a yellow melon.

After that, everything that was not my cat went
to sleep without a peep.

But I sat up in bed with worries in my head,
where was Greyling?

Suddenly from the top of my cupboard,
a stirring, it was Greyling purring ....
And in one giant bound he landed on my bed ...
and was found!

I've found my cat, so round, so cute,
so yellow, black and white.
Now, my friends, it's time to sleep. Good night!

2011 Award-winning Canadian Children's Books

Dear Reader: Here are some other great Canadian children's books. The ones with a star (★) are suitable for readers ages 4 to 7.

ALBERTA CHILDREN'S BOOK OF THE YEAR AWARD
★ Victor Lethbridge. *Little Chief and Mighty Gopher: The Pemmican Frenzy*. Illustrated by Ben Crane. Rolling Hills, AB: Storyteller Media and Tatanka Productions, 2010.

ALCUIN SOCIETY AWARDS FOR EXCELLENCE IN BOOK DESIGN IN CANADA
★ Cybèle Young. *A Few Blocks*. Designer: Michael Solomon. Toronto: Groundwood Books, 2011.

AMELIA FRANCES HOWARD-GIBBON ILLUSTRATOR'S AWARD
★ Marie-Louise Gay. *Roslyn Rutabaga and the Biggest Hole on Earth!* Toronto: Groundwood Books, 2010.

ANN CONNOR BRIMER AWARD FOR CHILDREN'S LITERATURE
Valerie Sherrard. *The Glory Wind*. Markham, ON: Fitzhenry & Whiteside, 2010.

ARTHUR ELLIS BEST JUVENILE CRIME AWARD
Alice Kuipers. *The Worst Thing She Ever Did*. Toronto: HarperTrophyCanada, 2010.

BLUE SPRUCE AWARD
★ Dave Whamond. *My Think-a-ma-Jink*. Toronto: Owlkids, 2010.

BOLEN BOOKS CHILDREN'S BOOK PRIZE
★ Kristi Bridgeman. *Uirapurú: Based on a Brazilian Legend* by P.K. Page. Fernie, BC: Oolichan Books, 2010.

CANADIAN LIBRARY ASSOCIATION BOOK OF THE YEAR FOR CHILDREN AWARD
Kenneth Oppel. *Half Brother*. Toronto: HarperCollins Publishers, 2010.

CANADIAN LIBRARY ASSOCIATION YOUNG ADULT CANADIAN BOOK AWARD
Kenneth Oppel. *Half Brother*. Toronto: HarperCollins Publishers, 2010.

CBA LIBRIS AWARD
★ (Picture Book) Helaine Becker. *A Porcupine in a Pine Tree: A Canadian 12 Days of Christmas*. Illustrated by Werner Zimmermann. Toronto: North Winds Press/ Scholastic, 2010.
(Young Readers) Sheree Fitch. *Pluto's Ghost*. Toronto: Doubleday Canada, 2010.

CHOCOLATE LILY YOUNG READERS' CHOICE AWARD
★ (Picture Book) Cynthia Nugent. *Fred and Pete at the Beach*. Victoria: Orca Book Publishers, 2009.
(Chapter Book) Kristin Butcher. *Zach and Zoe: Bully and the Beagle*. Toronto: James Lorimer, 2009.
(Novel) Iain Lawrence. *The Giant-Slayer*. New York: Delacorte Press, 2009.

CHRISTIE HARRIS ILLUSTRATED CHILDREN'S LITERATURE PRIZE
★ Julie Flett. *Owls See Clearly at Night: A Michif Alphabet*. Vancouver: Simply Read Books, 2010.

DIAMOND WILLOW AWARD
L.M. Falcone. *The Midnight Curse*. Toronto: Kids Can Press, 2010.

ELIZABETH MRAZIK-CLEAVER AWARD
★ Cybèle Young. *A Few Blocks*. Toronto: Groundwood Books, 2011.

FIRST NATION COMMUNITIES READ
Christy Jordan-Fenton and Margaret Pokiak-Fenton. *Fatty Legs: A True Story*. Illustrated by Liz Amini-Holmes. Toronto: Annick Press, 2010.

GEOFFREY BILSON AWARD FOR HISTORICAL FICTION FOR YOUNG PEOPLE
Valerie Sherrard. *The Glory Wind*. Markham, ON: Fitzhenry & Whiteside, 2010.

GOLDEN EAGLE CHILDREN'S CHOICE BOOK AWARD
The Brothers Armfinnigan (Dave Armstrong). *Adventures with Ploox*. Indianapolis: Dog Ear Publishing, 2011.

GOLDEN OAK AWARD
Rona Arato. *Courage and Compassion: Ten Canadians Who Made a Difference*. Toronto: Maple Tree Press, 2008.

GOVERNOR GENERAL'S LITERARY AWARDS
★ (Illustration) Cybèle Young. *Ten Birds*. Toronto: Kids Can Press, 2011.
(Text) Christopher Moore. *From Then to Now: A Short History of the World*. Illustrated by Andrej Krystoforski. Toronto: Tundra Books, 2011.

HACKMATACK CHILDREN'S CHOICE BOOK AWARD
(English Fiction) Ashley Spires. *Binky the Space Cat*. Toronto: Kids Can Press, 2009.
(English Non-Fiction) Valerie Wyatt. *How to Build Your Own Country*. Illustrated by Fred Rix. Toronto: Kids Can Press, 2009.

HELEN AND STAN VINE CANADIAN JEWISH BOOK AWARDS
Judie Oron. *Cry of the Giraffe*. Toronto: Annick Press, 2010.

INFORMATION BOOK AWARD
Tanya Lloyd Kyi. *50 Burning Questions: A Sizzling History of Fire*. Illustrated by Ross Kinnaird. Toronto: Annick Press, 2010.

JOE SHUSTER COMICS FOR KIDS AWARD
Scott Chantler. *Tower of Treasure*. Toronto: Kids Can Press, 2010.

JOHN SPRAY MYSTERY AWARD
Y.S. Lee. *A Spy in the House*. Somerville, MA: Candlewick Press, 2010.

LILLIAN SHEPHERD MEMORIAL AWARD FOR EXCELLENCE IN ILLUSTRATION
★ Susan Tooke. *The City Speaks in Drums* by Shauntay Grant. Halifax: Nimbus Publishing, 2010.

MANITOBA YOUNG READERS' CHOICE AWARD
Norah McClintock. *Taken*. Victoria: Orca Book Publishers, 2009.

MARILYN BAILLIE PICTURE BOOK AWARD
★ Laurel Croza. *I Know Here*. Illustrated by Matt James. Toronto: Groundwood Books, 2010.

McNALLY ROBINSON BOOK FOR YOUNG PEOPLE AWARD
(Young Adult) Maureen Fergus. *Ortega*. Toronto: Kids Can Press, 2010.

MUNICIPAL CHAPTER OF TORONTO IODE JEAN THROOP BOOK AWARD
Anna Kerz. *Better Than Weird*. Victoria: Orca Book Publishers, 2011.

NATIONAL CHAPTER OF CANADA IODE VIOLET DOWNEY BOOK AWARD
Virginia Frances Schwartz. *Crossing to Freedom*. Toronto: Scholastic Canada, 2010.

NORMA FLECK AWARD FOR CANADIAN CHILDREN'S NON-FICTION
Susan Hughes. *Case Closed? Nine Mysteries Unlocked by Modern Science*. Illustrated by Michael Wandelmaier. Toronto: Kids Can Press, 2010.

QUEBEC WRITERS' FEDERATION PRIZE FOR CHILDREN'S AND YOUNG ADULT LITERATURE
Alan Silberberg. *Milo: Sticky Notes and Brain Freeze*. New York: Aladdin, 2010.

R. ROSS ANNETT AWARD FOR CHILDREN'S LITERATURE
Deidre Anne Martin. *The Elegant Cockroach*. Illustrated by Stefanie Augustine. Calgary: Uppercase Publishing, 2010.

RED CEDAR BOOK AWARD
(Fiction) Alma Fullerton. *Libertad*. Markham, ON: Fitzhenry & Whiteside, 2008.
(Non-Fiction) Frieda Wishinsky and Elizabeth MacLeod. *Everything but the Kitchen Sink: Weird Stuff You Didn't Know About Food*. Illustrated by Travis King. New York: Scholastic Inc., 2008.

RED MAPLE AWARD
(Fiction) Vicki Grant. *Not Suitable for Family Viewing*. Toronto: HarperTrophyCanada, 2009.
(Non-Fiction) Mariatu Kamara with Susan McClelland. *The Bite of the Mango*. Toronto: Annick Press, 2009.

ROCKY MOUNTAIN BOOK AWARD
Seán Cullen. *The Prince of Neither Here Nor There*. Toronto: Puffin Canada, 2009.

RUTH AND SYLVIA SCHWARTZ CHILDREN'S BOOK AWARD
★ (Picture Book) Mélanie Watt. *Chester's Masterpiece*. Toronto: Kids Can Press, 2010.
(YA-Middle Reader) Kenneth Oppel. *Half Brother*. Toronto: HarperCollins Publishers, 2010.

SASKATCHEWAN BOOK AWARD
Adele Dueck. *Racing Home*. Regina: Coteau Books, 2011.

SCIENCE IN SOCIETY BOOK AWARD
Tanya Lloyd Kyi. *50 Poisonous Questions: A Book with Bite*. Illustrated by Ross Kinnaird. Toronto: Annick Press, 2011.

SHEILA A. EGOFF CHILDREN'S LITERATURE PRIZE
Maggie de Vries. *Hunger Journeys*. Toronto: HarperTrophyCanada, 2010.

SHINING WILLOW AWARD
★ Kenneth Oppel. *The King's Taster*. Illustrated by Steve Johnson and Lou Fancher. New York: HarperCollins Publishers, 2009.

SILVER BIRCH AWARD
(Express) Ashley Spires. *Binky the Space Cat*. Toronto: Kids Can Press, 2009.
(Fiction) Kevin Sylvester. *Neil Flambé and the Marco Polo Murders*. Toronto: Key Porter Books, 2010.
(Non-Fiction) Valerie Wyatt. *How to Build Your Own Country*. Illustrated by Fred Rix. Toronto: Kids Can Press, 2009.

SNOW WILLOW AWARD
Susin Nielsen. *Dear George Clooney, Please Marry My Mom*. Toronto: Tundra Books, 2010.

STELLAR BOOK AWARD
Kelley Armstrong. *The Summoning*. Toronto: Doubleday Canada, 2008.

SUNBURST AWARD FOR EXCELLENCE IN CANADIAN LITERATURE OF THE FANTASTIC
Paul Glennon. *Bookweirder*. Toronto: Doubleday Canada, 2010.

TD CANADIAN CHILDREN'S LITERATURE AWARD
Erin Bow. *Plain Kate*. Toronto: Scholastic Canada, 2011.

WHITE PINE AWARD
Richard Scarsbrook. *The Monkeyface Chronicles*. Saskatoon: Thistledown Press, 2010.

Philippe Beha

Philippe Beha is a greatly talented and renowned artist and a leading figure in Quebec children's literature. He graduated from the Beaux Arts de Strasbourg in France and arrived in Montreal in 1976. He worked for two years as a visual designer at Télé-Québec and has been a freelance illustrator since 1978. Philippe has illustrated close to 170 children's books for some thirty publishing houses both here and abroad. He is also very active in editorial, advertising and commercial illustration in Canada, the U.S. and Europe.

For Philippe, illustration is like cooking: He likes to blend textures, shapes and colours and to serve everything up with originality. "You have to know how to surprise yourself before surprising others. Everything is a matter of passion." His work, both exuberant and original, stands out on its own amidst Canada's children's literature landscape.

Philippe Beha's extraordinary talent and tireless creativity have been recognized on numerous occasions: The artist received the Canada Council for the Arts award and the Alvine-Bélisle award in 1983 for the illustrations in *Little Bear Can't Sleep, Peepee in the Potty, Don't Cut My Hair* and *I Love My Babysitter*; the Governor General's Literary Award for *Jeux de Pic-Mots* in 1988; the Mr. Christie's Book Award for the country's best Francophone illustrated children's book in 1990 for *What do the fairies do with all those teeth*?; and the Québec/Wallonie-Bruxelles children's literature award in 2005 for his illustrations in *Les Devinettes d'Henriette* by Henriette Major. In 2006, his book *Pas si bête*, for which he created the text and illustrations, received the Prix du livre jeunesse des bibliothèques de Montréal. *Les Pays inventés* (text by Henriette Major) won the illustration prize of the Trois-Rivières Salon du livre in 2008.

J'ai perdu mon chat was also a finalist in the Prix du livre jeunesse des bibliothèques de Montréal in 2009.